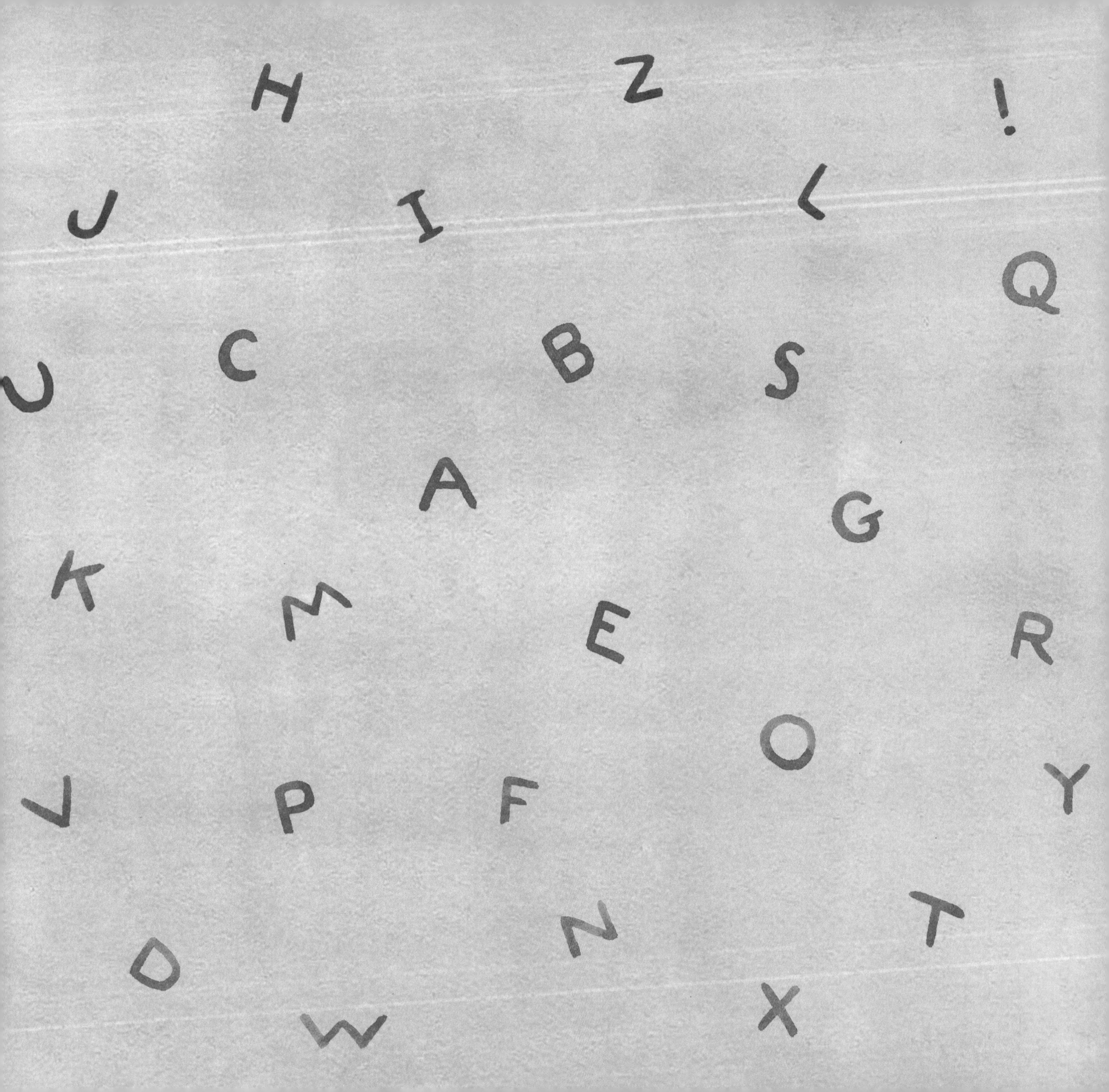
H Z !
J I L Q
U C B S
A G
K M E R
O
V P F Y
N T
D W X

BY JULIE LARIOS AND JULIE PASCHKIS

PEACHTREE
ATLANTA

Published by
PEACHTREE PUBLISHING COMPANY INC.
1700 Chattahoochee Avenue
Atlanta, Georgia 30318-2112
www.peachtree-online.com

Edited by Vicky Holifield
Design and composition by Julie Paschkis and Adela Pons

Illustrations painted with India ink and gouache on 100% rag hot press archival watercolor paper

Printed in December 2019 by Tien Wah Press in Malaysia
10 9 8 7 6 5 4 3 2 1
First Edition
ISBN 978-1-68263-169-0

Cataloging-in-Publication Data is available from the Library of Congress.

THIS JOURNEY IS FOR JACKSON
WHOOP-DE-DO!
—JULIE LARIOS

AND OF COURSE FOR EEK:
ERIC ERNST KAYE
—JULIE PASCHKIS

A
achoo

bzzz
B

chirp
C

ding-a-ling
D

Eeek!

fwump
F

grrr
G

harrumph
H

J
jring-jring
ick
I

kabonk
K

L
lalala

M
maaaah

N
num-num

O
oops

P
plop

quack
Q

R
rah-rah

sis-boom-bah
S

ta-da
T

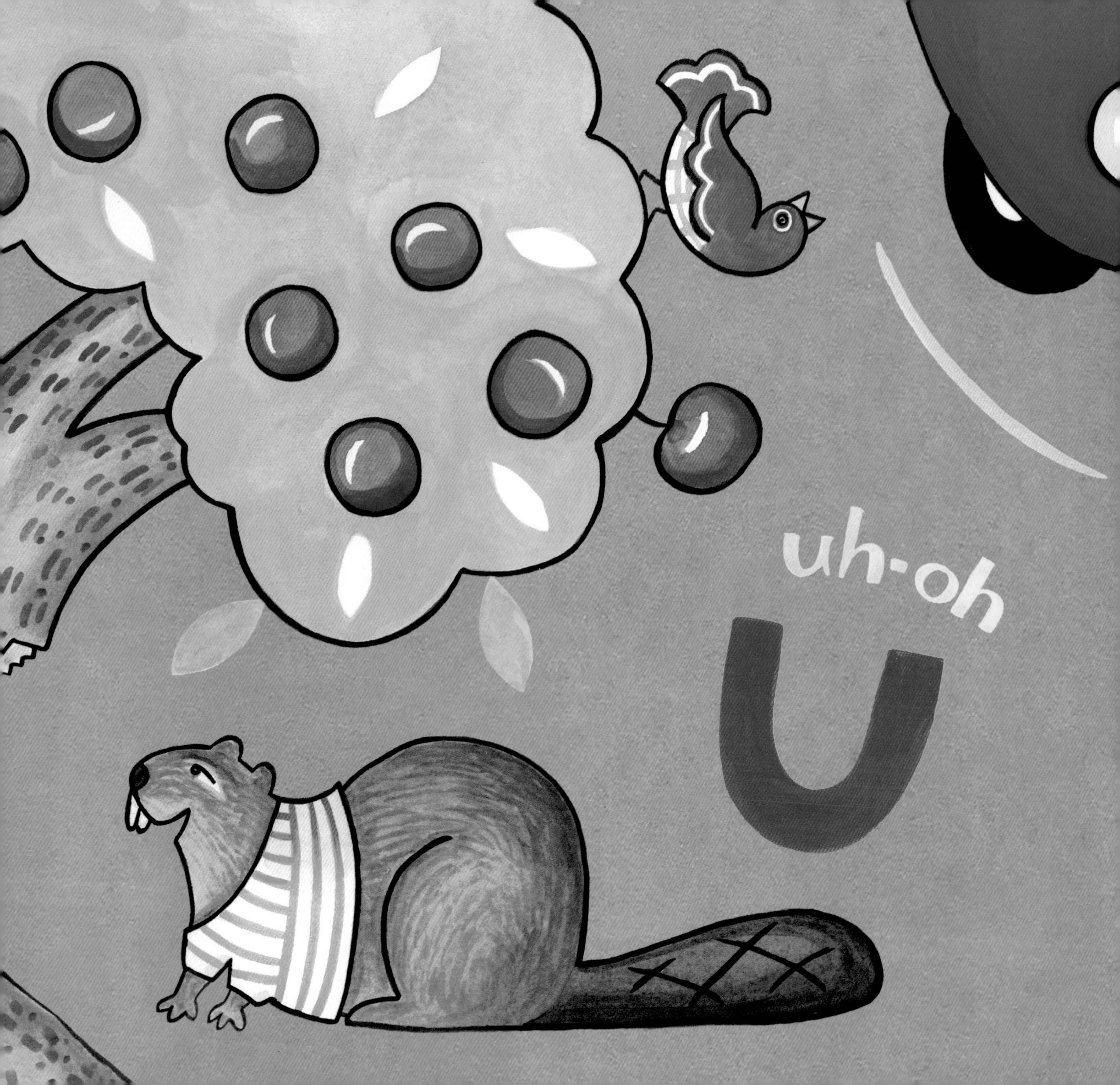
uh-oh
U

varoom
V

whee
W

X xoxoxo

Y
yahoo

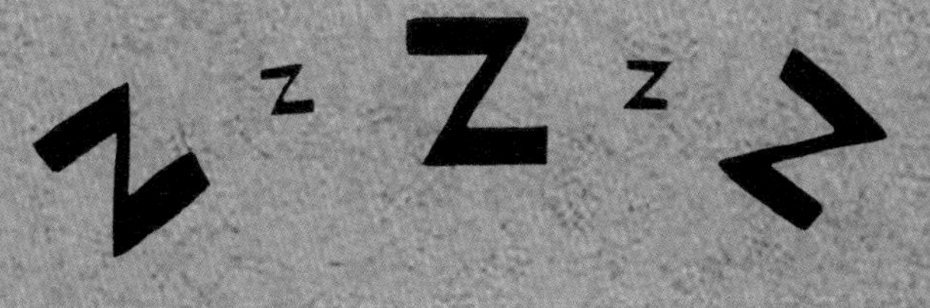

Z

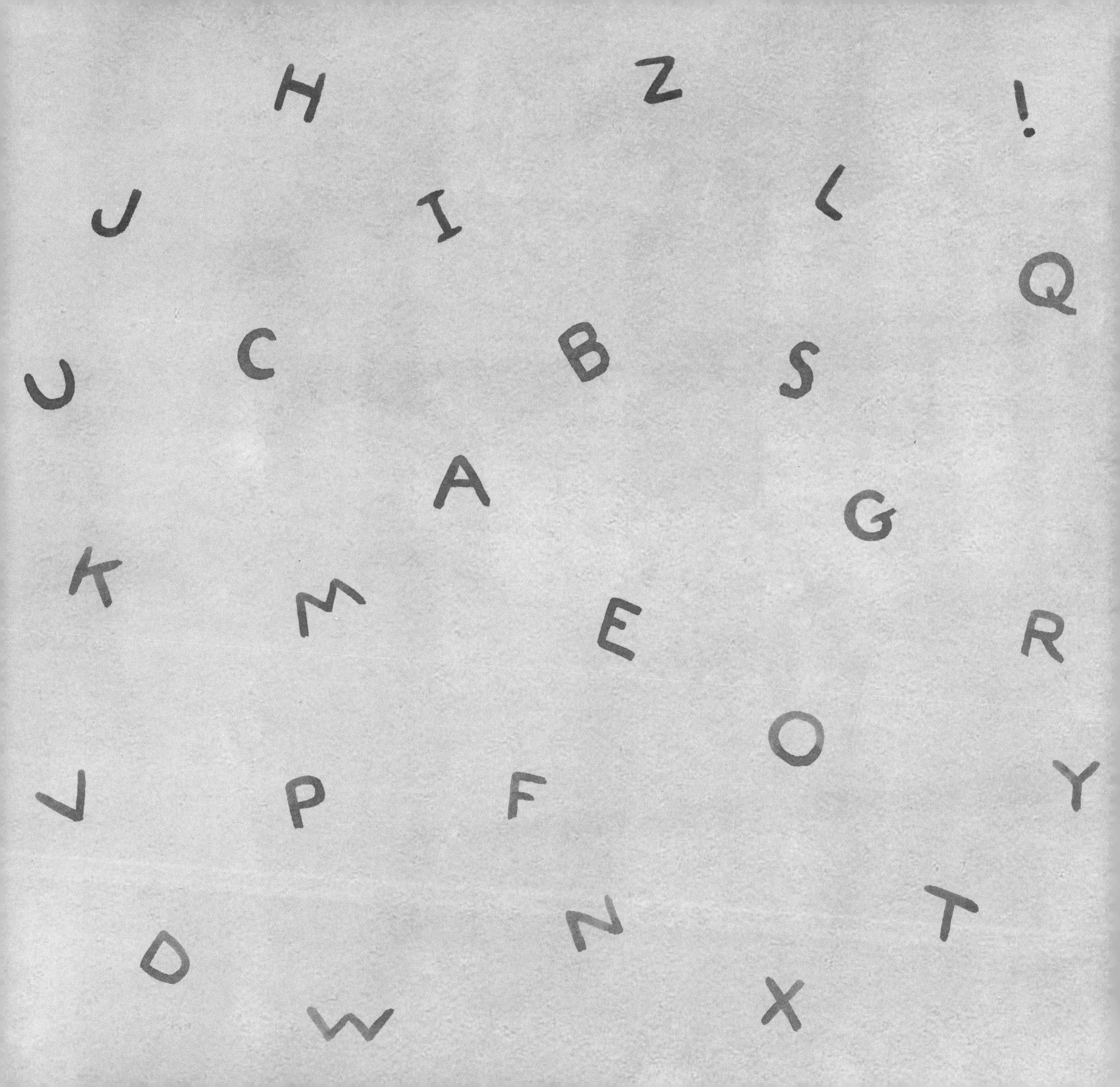
H
Z
!
J
I
L
Q
U
C
B
S
A
G
K
M
E
R
O
V
P
F
Y
T
N
D
X
W

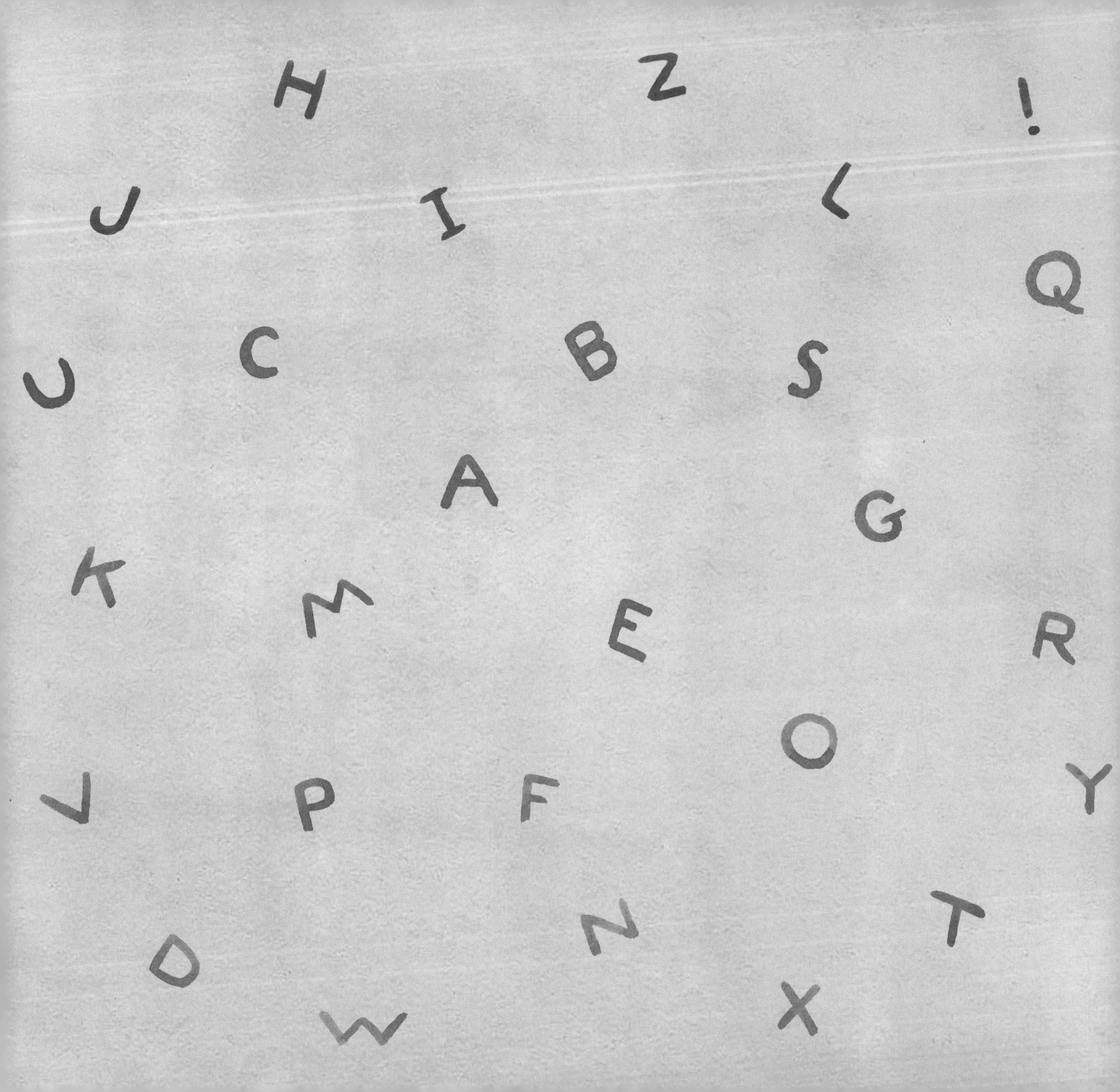